Samuel French Acting Edition

Who is Theo?

by David L. Kimple

SAMUELFRENCH.COM   SAMUELFRENCH.CO.UK

FOR PRODUCTION ENQUIRIES

UNITED STATES AND CANADA
Info@SamuelFrench.com
1-866-598-8449

UNITED KINGDOM AND EUROPE
Plays@SamuelFrench.co.uk
020-7255-4302

Each title is subject to availability from Samuel French, depending upon country of performance. Please be aware that *WHO IS THEO?* may not be licensed by Samuel French in your territory. Professional and amateur producers should contact the nearest Samuel French office or licensing partner to verify availability.

MUSIC USE NOTE

IMPORTANT BILLING AND CREDIT REQUIREMENTS

WHO IS THEO? was first presented at Bristol Valley Theater in Naples, New York on June 25, 2015 by the Friends of Bristol Valley Playhouse and Executive Artistic Director Karin Bowersock. The production was directed by David E. Shane, with sets by Tim McMath, costumes by Samantha J. Miller, lights by Daniel Winters, props by Jarrett Fernald, and sound by Adam Bintz. The Stage Manager was Josh Lau; the Assistant to the Director was Kendyl Litwiller; the Assistant Stage Manager was Daniel Parker. The cast was as follows:

DONNA.. Sara Fetgatter

ELLIE .... Lauren Weinberg

THEO .... André Torquato

JAMIE ....Steven Smith

OFFICER PERKINS.............................. Chris J. Handley

OFFICER BART........................Kate Muñoz / Devon Adams

WHO IS THEO? (one-act version) was commissioned by the Off-Broadway Players at the University of Massachusetts-Lowell and presented as a workshop production in the Festival of Change in April of 2013.

CHARACTERS

DONNA – Female. Mid-late twenties. Assistant at a Law Firm. Driven, intelligent, hungry for more. Any Ethnicity.

ELLIE – Female. Mid-late twenties. Writer. Playful, young-hearted, spontaneous. Any Ethnicity.

JAMIE – Male. 32. Costume Designer. Driven, focused, not messing around. Any Ethnicity.

THEO – Male. Mid-late twenties/early thirties. Fashion Management. Lovable, playful, smart, handsome. Any Ethnicity.

OFFICER PERKINS – Male or Female. Rookie Cop. Nervous, scared, blinded by fear. Any Ethnicity.

OFFICER BART – Offstage Voice Only. Seasoned Cop. Any Ethnicity.

SETTING

Queens, NY

TIME

Present Day

AUTHOR'S NOTE

"—" should function rhythmically as a silent line.

SPECIAL THANKS

Special thanks to: David E. Shane, Karin Bowersock, Bristol Valley Theater, University of Massachusetts-Lowell, Catie Humphreys, Courtney Alana Ward, Elizabeth Burton, Justin Bowen, Michael Fatica, Kris Thorpe, David McElwee, Blaine Johnston, and my brilliant Family.

ACT I

(A cozy three bedroom apartment in one of the boroughs of New York. It has a decent size to it. There are at least four visible doors inside the apartment: front door, bedroom door#1, bedroom door#2, bedroom door#3.)

(DONNA comes in the front door. She does not see that ELLIE is laying on the floor, drunkenly wearing various shades of green and St. Patrick's Day decorations.)

ELLIE. I can't get up.

DONNA. AH! Oh my god!

ELLIE. Ah! *(laughs hysterically)*

DONNA. I had no idea you were there. Ah! Stop laughing. You scared me half to death.

ELLIE. You're so jumpy. I didn't even do anything and you 'bout lost your pants!

DONNA. I'm super jittery. I've had way too much frickin' coffee. I'll be up 'til Easter.

(Over the course of DONNA's rant she should make it in and out of bedroom door #1, closing it behind her. Perhaps to change into her pajamas.)

The office was hell today and then I had to dodge about a million friggin' leprechauns on the train. I hate this stupid day. I saw three-three girls throwing up before I even went underground. Then YOU-UGH. I assumed you and Jamie were in bed.

ELLIE. I just got home.

DONNA. What are you drunk?

ELLIE. Jamie left already.

1

DONNA. Already? He didn't even say bye? I haven't seen him in three days.

ELLIE. He might be still here still but he might be finally sleeping too but we wouldn't want to wake the dragon. But I'm pretty sure he left this morning. I had beers to whiskeys. The world is spinning. I'm dying.

DONNA. You're not dying.

ELLIE. If I die young then everyone will remember my untapped potential instead of my failure.

DONNA. You're not dying. No one is going to die tonight.

ELLIE. Promise?

DONNA. Promise. You're basically the most successful person I know; your potential is not untapped. If you die, then that is what you get for going out on St. Patrick's Day as if it's a real holiday.

ELLIE. It is a real holiday. It is to me and my people. I just needed to take a break from editing.

DONNA. Your people?

ELLIE. The Irish. I'll be fine. I have until 5 to finish.

DONNA. You're not Irish. PM or AM?

ELLIE. Or come up with a new story. PM. Or throw the whole thing and myself off the Empire State building. The Irish is in me blood. Donna, it's so bad!

DONNA. You grew up in Jacksonville. What's bad?

ELLIE. My family is from Ireland.

DONNA. You're not Irish. The book is good.

ELLIE. I'm allowed to say that I am Ire-lish. You read it? You read it?

DONNA. Well, I haven't yet –

ELLIE. UGH. Then what do I say?

DONNA. To whom?

ELLIE. About my heritage?

DONNA. American.

ELLIE. I think you're wrong. I asked you to read and you didn't and now it's terrible. Let's have a drink.

DONNA. I think you spent the day drinking green beer from a plastic cup on East 27th street and don't have a right to an opinion. No more drinks. Go to sleep. I need to be alone. I need to mellow. I'm shaking.

ELLIE. And I'm dying.

DONNA. You're so drunk I can smell you. Sober up. What time are you getting up to work?

ELLIE. Not for awhile. Sssiieven? Seven? Seven. Oh my god. Seven. Plenty of time.

DONNA. That's five hours from now.

ELLIE. Oh my god.

DONNA. Good luck with that. god you smell bad.

ELLIE. I don't wanna. I smell like roses.

DONNA. You smell like Second Avenue.

ELLIE. Are you mad at me?

DONNA. No I'm really tired but completely tweaked on coffee. Superlatively tweaked. Most tweaked.

ELLIE. It's too late for Irish coffee.

DONNA. Colombian. Shut up. I have to have it or I lose my edge and seem weak. Ellie, she actually called me weak today. Normally she says it behind my back. Today she said it to my face. No bull. She stopped just said, "You're weak."

ELLIE. Booooooo! I thought you were good at your job.

DONNA. I am! I'm wonderful at my job. You need water, aspirin and to get in bed. Go to bed.

> (**ELLIE** *gathers herself up but, goes to the fridge and opens a beer.*)

DONNA. We can't keep doing things the way we've been doing them. Being lazy. I should go back to the office. I think I'm going to get fired.

ELLIE. You're not going to get fired. Sit down.

DONNA. I just want to be happy and drunk like you.

ELLIE. Think of happy thoughts. At least you have snuggly boy to keep your warm.

DONNA. Yeah sure he's fine I guess. He's busy with stuff. There is this new project or an old project or I don't even know what he really does really.

ELLIE. You don't really like him that much do you?

DONNA. No I do. Yeah, yeah. I'm fine. He's always busy. I get that. I'm busy. We're easy peasey. I guess. It's just blah. Blah. Everything is blah.

ELLIE. Why are you spazzing? You're spazzing.

DONNA. Because.

ELLIE. Because what? What do you want?

DONNA. I don't know. Everything.

ELLIE. You want everything? Everything what?

DONNA. To be different.

ELLIE. Different how?

DONNA. Everything that I'm doing.

ELLIE. Specifically. Like what?

DONNA. Absolutely everything. Okay! It's this friggin' job.

ELLIE. You like your job.

DONNA. I *don't*. I'm supposed to because it's supposed to be great and blah blah and I'm supposed to be happy that I'm not homeless and hungry but I don't like it.

ELLIE. Do you?

DONNA. Why are you pschiatristing me?

ELLIE. Shh! Think of me as a friend.

DONNA. You are my friend-what?

ELLIE. Relax. What about your job is troubling you?

DONNA. It's beneath me. I don't mean to be a queen, but I am better than filing and errands.

ELLIE. Let's talk more about that.

DONNA. I just am. I passed the bar. That is a hard thing to do but I'm in this entry-level place.

ELLIE. Yes. Tell me more about that experience.

DONNA. Oh my god. I passed the bar. I'm wasting my life.

ELLIE. How?

DONNA. By being an assistant. I don't want to talk about this anymore. It's depressing me. I'm sorry I said anything.

ELLIE. It's a stepping stone.

DONNA. It's bullhonky.

ELLIE. It's a good job.

DONNA. Drop it. I mean it, El. I don't even know what I'm complaining about. I'm just in the worst mood. Nothing is happening.

ELLIE. That's all in your head. Just take it day by day. Eventually –

DONNA. I don't want eventually. I want now. Now.

ELLIE. NOW is 2 a.m. with a beer at the dinner table. You're missing your actual life because you're obsessing about stuff you can't control right now.

DONNA. Whatever. You're freaking out too. You're just avoiding your problem.

ELLIE. Just because my book is the worst most awful thing I've ever written doesn't mean I'm freaking out.

I'm drunk and happy! See? Laughing.

DONNA. I don't want to talk about it.

ELLIE. You're freaking out. Enjoy this beer with me –

DONNA. Drop it!

ELLIE. —

I'm thinking about starting this new thing. It's a blog series that uses the deterioration of fruit as a metaphor for societal expectations. I think to myself "That's sort of interesting." But it isn't. It's typical. It's crap. But I have to imagine that stuff because it is part of the process. We have to trust the process. Like Jamie! Unlike you, he's already old. Almost thirty-two and is only now making it to the big leagues. He locks himself at his desk all the time and nitpicks every angle and swatch because it's part of the process. He's been awake for almost three days straight and now he's on his way to Chicago to design this show and then he'll finally be working on big flashy Broadway.

DONNA. And you're probably going to win a Pulitzer and I'll still be stuck in the mail room.

ELLIE. Is there really a mail room?

DONNA. Jamie better hate Chicago. Did he really leave without saying goodbye?

ELLIE. He was def leaving today or tomorrow.

DONNA. I thought you said yesterday? I don't want a new roommate. Make him come back.

ELLIE. He has to go and we'll have a new roomie for a little while and we'll be great. He will hate Chicago. All you can do is keep on keepin' on. We're doing what we can while we can with what we can and who we can and yes we can –

DONNA. YES we cancan.

ELLIE. Yeah!

DONNA. —

ELLIE. I have to go to sleeps now.

DONNA. I think so. Up! Time for bed.

ELLIE. Okay.

DONNA. What time in the morning?

ELLIE. Seven.

DONNA. Go to bed.

ELLIE. Give yourself some time to succeed.

DONNA. Please just go to sleep.

ELLIE. Are you hearing me?

DONNA. Yes. I hear you.

ELLIE. Okay.

DONNA. Okay. Shut up.

ELLIE. Just start there, okay? I love you.

DONNA. Love you too.

ELLIE. G'night, fettuccine monkey.

DONNA. Kiss Noise.

(**ELLIE** *goes into door #2.* **DONNA** *sits on the couch. She opens a casebook and flips through* *some pages. Maybe she flips through the channels on the TV too. She hears one of the bedroom doors open.* **THEO**, *a handsome but messy and very intoxicated man dressed as a leprechaun, comes out of door #1.)*

DONNA. Go back to bed. I'm trying to read. Sorry, not your stuff. Sorry. But I promise once I finish the last of this –

THEO. Youz a avid reader.

DONNA. Whoa! Leprechaun! AH! What the – who are you?!

THEO. Who?

DONNA. Who are you? What are you doing in my apartment?

THEO. I'm Thee –

DONNA. What? Get out! Thee?

THEO. Thee ugh.

DONNA. Thee? What? Who? What? What?

THEO. Theo.

DONNA. Stand back! I'll scream.

THEO. Don't scream.

DONNA. AHH!

THEO. It's late. That's loud.

DONNA. Who are you?

THEO. Theo.

DONNA. Who?

THEO. I'm a leprechaun.

DONNA. Who?

THEO. Still Theo.

DONNA. Get out. Where did you come from? Why are you in my apartment?

THEO. I – Um –

DONNA. Answer me. Where did you come from? Who are you?

THEO. I –

DONNA. Come on.

THEO. I –

DONNA. Who are you?

THEO. Shut up!

DONNA. Don't you take that tone with me!

THEO. Sorry.

DONNA. Where were you?

THEO. My room.

DONNA. Your room?

THEO. Over there.

DONNA. Where?

THEO. The room.

DONNA. What? Wait. Holy cow, are you the sublet? Are you Jamie's sublet?

THEO. Mmmm –

DONNA. I almost rape-whistled you. You scared the crap out of me.

THEO. Yeah.

DONNA. My heart is racing.

THEO. Mine too.

DONNA. So much friggin' coffee. Ouch! I hate this stupid day. Friggin' crazy drunk people. UGH!

Okay. I'm Donna. Ellie, she's the other roomie, just went to bed.

THEO. Good times!

DONNA. …Are you okay?

THEO. Great. You?

DONNA. It's late. Have you been in the room this whole time?

THEO. I just got home. I hav'ta work tomorrow.

DONNA. You got a job already? What do you do?

THEO. Fassssshen.

DONNA. Fashion? You do fashion? You don't look like one of those fashion guys.

THEO. I look like a leprechaun.

DONNA. What do you do?

THEO. Leprechaun Couture.

DONNA. What?

THEO. What?

DONNA. What?

THEO. I'll take the train.

DONNA. Oh. You're hammered aren't you?

THEO. You are too.

DONNA. No I'm not.

THEO. Seems like it.

DONNA. It's just the coffee.

THEO. But it's St. Patrick's Day.

DONNA. And you think you're Irish.

THEO. Yeah! How'd you know?

DONNA. You're not Irish.

THEO. I'm Irish-American.

DONNA. American. Irish descent.

THEO. I'm a leprechaun.

DONNA. Sure.

THEO. I grant wishes.

DONNA. I wish you really did.

THEO. What do you wish for?

DONNA. Don't even get me started.

THEO. I want a puppy.

DONNA. I do love puppies.

THEO. An English bull-terrier.

DONNA. Which one is that?

THEO. They have faces like this –

(impersonates an English bull terrier)

DONNA. You're good at that.

THEO. WOOF!

DONNA. You're really drunk.

THEO. Yes and I'm totally exhausted but I accidentally coked out and my head won't stop.

DONNA. I'm sorry, what?

THEO. I was waiting for the bathroom and I turned around and my nose breathed in some coke.

DONNA. Okay –

THEO. I didn't try to though.

DONNA. Sure.

THEO. It was a cokerape!

DONNA. What?

THEO. I'm not some druggie.

DONNA. Someone raped you on coke?

THEO. Cokeraped.

DONNA. This isn't funny. You can't joke about that.

THEO. No ha ha's.

DONNA. I think it's time for bed.

THEO. It was *coke*rape not raperape.

DONNA. That doesn't make any more sense now than it did before.

THEO. I was waiting to pee and someone was all "Coke?" and I was wasted and I was all "Noke" and then I turned my face away and then I turned my face back and I was inhaling and there was a hand up near my face and it had coke on it and I breathed it in. I didn't try to do it. It was just there and I breathed it in because of my nose. And now I'm just another coked out leprechaun looking for love in all the wrong places.

Don't look at me. I'm so ashamed.

DONNA. Okay wastecase, maybe chug some water and pass out then.

THEO. How much?

DONNA. About half a gallon.

THEO. Okay. Hold my hat.

(**THEO** *puts his head under the sink and schlurps.*)

DONNA. Okay. Goodnight.

(THEO *walks towards* DONNA *on the couch and settles in next to her. He puts his head on her lap.*)

DONNA. Oh, oh, okay. Hi there…man. You are a man on my lap now. I didn't mean pass out on me.

THEO. You're soft like a pillow.

DONNA. Well you're drunk. Rude.

THEO. You smell nice.

DONNA. It's Tom Ford.

THEO. It's good. I like you a lot.

DONNA. It cost like two hundred bucks. You better.

THEO. I really like you so hard.

DONNA. Thank you.

THEO. Welcomes.

DONNA. —

—

(DONNA *pets his hair and tries to go with it.*)

DONNA. Are you wearing glitter? Um. Are you asleep? Hello?

THEO. What?

DONNA. What is your name again?

THEO. Theodore Forbes McGuintilly. You're really pretty.

DONNA. Thanks.

THEO. You have no idea how pretty you are and I can tell. You're gorgeous. You could model.

DONNA. Yeah right.

THEO. Print. You could do print. You're not tall.

DONNA. So.

THEO. D'you model?

DONNA. No.

THEO. Then I'm right. You really don't know how pretty you are.

DONNA. Thank you, Theo. You are also very – handsome. Even as a leprechaun.

THEO. Duh.

DONNA. And you seem to know it.

THEO. So what? I'm allowed to know that I'm handsome and you're allowed to know that you're beautiful, babe.

DONNA. Do not call me babe. I am not your babe.

THEO. And funny. And probably smart. What do you do?

DONNA. I'm an assistant at a law firm.

THEO. Lawyer.

DONNA. No. Nope. Just said assistant.

THEO. That's what you want to be?

DONNA. Yeah right. Nobody aspires to be an assistant. You know how it goes. There is a hierarchy. I'm at the bottom of the barrel for now but eventually, probably soon, I'll get promoted. I haven't really been doing it that long so – It really isn't the dream. Not the end point. But it is my field.

THEO. What do you really want to be in the end?

DONNA. A lawyer.

THEO. So why do you assist?

DONNA. It takes time to get there.

THEO. But what if you don't ever get there? You could die today and you'd die an assistant.

DONNA. Are you threatening me.

THEO. No. It's a 'live your life to the fullest' kind of thing.

DONNA. Don't threaten me.

THEO. Not threatening but just imagine – you could get shot tonight and you would still be –

DONNA. Why would I get shot? Do you have a gun? Are you one of those unicorn right-wing New Yorkers? I knew they existed but I never thought I'd live with one –

THEO. I'm moderate. Just listen.

DONNA. Do you have a gun?

THEO. NO.

DONNA. Okay. What?

THEO. Do you love it? The job.

DONNA. Not really.

THEO. Oh. I don't like it when people don't love what they do. People who settle depress me.

DONNA. I'm not settling.

THEO. You don't love what you do.

DONNA. I don't love it exactly, but I know why I do it.

THEO. Why?

DONNA. Because –

THEO. Because why?

DONNA. Because it's one of the better firms in the city.

THEO. But you are not a lawyer.

DONNA. But I will be.

THEO. But when?

DONNA. Sometime.

THEO. Not now.

DONNA. Not yet.

THEO. Why not just go somewhere else and be now.

DONNA. I don't have the experience to –

THEO. Be the experience. Why do you need experience working as an assistant to do something that is nothing like being an assistant? Just say it is and it is.

For instance, I am a leprechaun.

DONNA. What?

THEO. I just said that I was and then I am.

DONNA. You're not actually a leprechaun.

THEO. How dare you! You just lost a wish.

DONNA. I'm just learning the system, Lucky.

THEO. You're being the little fish in the big pond but I don't understand why you don't go be the big fish.

DONNA. They have experience that I don't.

THEO. And you have things they don't have. How do you think they got to the pot of gold?

DONNA. What pot of gold?

THEO. I don't know jack about the law world, but they probably brought some new ideas to the table and got a little lucky and that helped to change the way things were done. Am I right? So why don't you be the big-fish leprechaun and do what you want to do? "If you build it, they will come."

DONNA. It's not that simple.

THEO. "Leap and the net will appear."

DONNA. I'm afraid of heights.

THEO. You're annoyed.

DONNA. Yep.

THEO. Why?

DONNA. Were you listening through the door earlier? Because I was talking about work stuff earlier and now you're interrogating me.

THEO. I wasn't.

DONNA. I don't believe you.

THEO. Then you have trust issues. I just like seeing people succeeding and being happy. That's what I do and I am super happy. So I don't see why it doesn't work for other people. I'm sorry. I probably don't make any sense. I'm really wasted.

DONNA. —

How long will you be living here?

THEO. I'm sorry. I really am.

DONNA. It's okay, just go to bed and sober up.

—

What?

THEO. What?

DONNA. Why are you looking at me like that?

THEO. I would like to kiss you. Would you like to kiss me?

DONNA. What? Why? No –

THEO. It will make me happy. You're beautiful –

DONNA. Thank you.

THEO. – and I deserve a pretty girl like you.

DONNA. That was cute. But you're tanked and I have a kind-of boyfriend and –

THEO. – you don't like me. Sadface.

DONNA. No I do. Weirdly enough I do kinda like you but I think it's time for you to go to sleep.

THEO. Smooches?

DONNA. No smooches.

THEO. Just a tiny smooch.

DONNA. No. No smooching.

THEO. Just a little one. I can tell you want to.

DONNA. Even if I want to, I'm not smooching you. We live together now and you're just so high. Go to bed.

THEO. Please, pretty? Pretty please? Please.

DONNA. Alright, stop whining.

> (**DONNA** *considers it and gives him a small kiss on the cheek. Okay.*)

That was just to hush you up.

THEO. Thank you.

DONNA. You're welcome. Never happening again.

THEO. Don't be foolish.

DONNA. Foolish? Realistic.

THEO. Let's be real.

DONNA. I'm being real. Even that was bad.

THEO. Bad but good.

DONNA. I already have guilt.

THEO. Why?

DONNA. Because. Now let's go to bed.

THEO. One kiss on the cheek and now we're going to bed.

DONNA. Not we. There is no we.

THEO. There could be.

DONNA. There could not be.

THEO. Why?

DONNA. Because of him.

THEO. Who?

DONNA. My guy.

THEO. Your guy.

DONNA. Yeah. Matt.

THEO. A mat is a thing not a name.

DONNA. True.

THEO. Double entendre.

DONNA. Not quite.

THEO. C'mere.

DONNA. No. Stop that.

THEO. You.

DONNA. No, you stop it. Stop that.

THEO. Why?

DONNA. Because it is weirdly kind of interesting and it's a little hard to say no.

THEO. I know.

DONNA. I know. So stop it.

THEO. Why?

DONNA. Stop seducing me.

THEO. You're seducing me.

DONNA. No! I'm stopping this.

THEO. Nope. You're making me fall in love with you.

DONNA. How? No I am not. Not on purpose. I'm a good person.

THEO. You are. I know you are.

DONNA. I try to be.

THEO. And you don't really care about doormat.

DONNA. Yeah I –

THEO. You're happy with him? He makes you happy?

DONNA. He's a good guy.

THEO. But you're not happy and the two of you aren't wonderful. Like us.

DONNA. There is no us, Theo.

THEO. There could be.

> *(**THEO** kisses **DONNA**.)*

THEO. Right?

> *(He goes to kiss her once more and **DONNA** almost lets it happen but instinctively smacks him in the face.)*

THEO. Sadface.

DONNA. Oh my god! I'm sorry.

THEO. Ouchie.

DONNA. I didn't mean to – It just – It just kind of happened.

THEO. You slapped my face.

DONNA. I did. I slapped your face.

THEO. You slapped me in my face.

DONNA. I slapped you in your face.

THEO. My handsome face.

DONNA. I'm sorry. What can I do?

THEO. Kiss it better?

DONNA. Okay.

Wait. No.

THEO. Yes. Please.

DONNA. No. Thank you.

THEO. Yes.

DONNA. No.

THEO. Yes.

DONNA. No. Stop.

THEO. No. You love it.

DONNA. No. I don't.

THEO. Yes. A little.

DONNA. Yes. A little.

THEO. Yes. A lot.

DONNA. No. We're done.

THEO. No. Just started.

DONNA. No. It's over.

THEO. Yes. For now.

DONNA. No. Forever.

THEO. Yes. Together Forever.

DONNA. No. That's enough.

THEO. No. Not enough.

DONNA. Yes. Too much.

THEO. No. A bit more.

DONNA. No. I won't.

THEO. Yes. For me.

DONNA. Yeah, yeah.

THEO. Yes! I knew it.

DONNA. No. That was sarcasm.

THEO. No. You said yeah.

DONNA. Yeah. I meant no.

THEO. No.

DONNA. Yes. Go to your room.

THEO. No. I don't want to.

DONNA. Yes, Theo.

THEO. No. I want to stay with you.

DONNA. Theodore Forbes McGuintilly, go to bed.

THEO. No.

DONNA. Yes. Look, I'm also going to bed.

THEO. Yes! With me?

DONNA. No. Let me put you to bed?

THEO. No.

DONNA. Yes.

THEO. No.

DONNA. I'm done.

THEO. No.

DONNA. —

THEO. Yes?

DONNA. —

THEO. YesNo?

DONNA. —

THEO. NoYes? YesNo? NONO? YesYes? Okay. Okaykay. Okay, but I'm doing this against my freedom.

DONNA. Understood. Loud and clear. Goodnight!

> *(DONNA escorts THEO to door #3. THEO kisses DONNA once more and goes inside. DONNA shuts the door.)*

Goodnight, Theo. Finally.

> *(DONNA notices that door #1 is open and shuts it before re-entering the living room to turn off the lights. The room is dark for a moment when shouting can be heard from a bedroom. DONNA runs back to the light switch.)*

> *(JAMIE comes out of door #3 in his PJ pants.)*

JAMIE. Who the eff are you? Who the –? What the –? Who the heck is that?

DONNA. What? Jamie? What?

JAMIE. What in the hell?

DONNA. You're home?

JAMIE. Yeah!

DONNA. I thought you were gone.

JAMIE. There is a dude in my bed.

DONNA. I'm so glad you're here.

JAMIE. I've got a guy in my bed.

DONNA. I have to tell you, this has been the weirdest night.

JAMIE. Man. In. My. Bed.

DONNA. OH.

JAMIE. YEAH.

DONNA. Nice. From where?

JAMIE. I don't know.

DONNA. Who is it?

JAMIE. I don't know. He's in my bed right now.

DONNA. Is that a bad thing?

JAMIE. Yes.

DONNA. Why?

JAMIE. I don't know who he is.

DONNA. Okay.

JAMIE. He just crawled into bed with me.

DONNA. When?

JAMIE. Literally just now. Passed out.

DONNA. That's weird.

JAMIE. I know.

DONNA. Where did he come from?

JAMIE. I don't know.

DONNA. Weird.

JAMIE. Weirder. I think he's dressed like a Leprechaun.

DONNA. OH!

JAMIE. What?

DONNA. It's Theo!

JAMIE. What?

DONNA. It's just Theo.

JAMIE. Who is Theo?

DONNA. Your sublet.

JAMIE. My sublet?

DONNA. That was scary for a minute. Your sublet Theo.

JAMIE. My sublet Theo?

DONNA. What a relief.

JAMIE. My sublet's name is Chaz.

DONNA. Chaz? What kind of a name is Chaz?

JAMIE. Just a name.

DONNA. Awful name.

JAMIE. Who cares?

DONNA. I do. I have to live with a 'Chaz'?

JAMIE. For like a month!

DONNA. When are you leaving?

JAMIE. Really early and I finally just fell asleep.

DONNA. Tomorrow?

JAMIE. Basically now.

DONNA. I was so mad, I thought you left and didn't say bye.

JAMIE. I'm still here.

DONNA. Don't leave.

JAMIE. Still here. Stranger in my bed.

DONNA. Oh yeah.

JAMIE. Who is that leprechaun in my bed?

DONNA. Theo.

JAMIE. Who is Theo?

DONNA. Your suble – OH!

—

I don't know!

JAMIE. Me neither.

—

DONNA & JAMIE. Ellie!

JAMIE. Did she bring him home?

DONNA. No. No way. I mean she was drinking a bit but she has to work early and she wasn't that drunk. A little dimmer than usual but she didn't bring anyone home for sure.

(**ELLIE** *comes bursting out of door #2.*)

ELLIE. Who died?!

DONNA. Who is Theo?

ELLIE. Who?

DONNA. Theo.

ELLIE. Who is Theo?

DONNA. Yeah.

ELLIE. I don't know who Theo is. Who is Theo?

DONNA. We are asking you.

ELLIE. I'm confused by the question.

JAMIE. Just who is he?

ELLIE. I need a context clue.

JAMIE. We don't know, Eleanor.

ELLIE. Why are we asking?

DONNA. There's a guy in Jamie's bed right now.

ELLIE. Oh good!

JAMIE. What?

ELLIE. 'Bout time one of us had an overnight guest.

JAMIE. No.

ELLIE. Overnight guest 2015! Yaaassss.*

DONNA. That's Theo.

ELLIE. Who?

DONNA. The overnight guest.

JAMIE. The guy in my bed.

ELLIE. How'd you meet him?

JAMIE. Who?

ELLIE. The guy. Theo.

DONNA. He didn't.

JAMIE. He just crawled into my bed.

ELLIE. And that is a problem?

JAMIE. He's not 'in my bed' in my bed, just physically. He's totally passed out.

ELLIE. Sorry, Jamie. Next time! You're so handsome.

JAMIE. Ellie, I didn't bring him home. He is in my bed and I did not bring him here.

(ELLIE *peeks into the bedroom.*)

ELLIE. He looks cute. Is he cute?

DONNA. Very cute.

JAMIE. I don't know, I was too alarmed by the stranger danger happening under my covers.

ELLIE. Stranger danger! Yes.

JAMIE. I haven't slept in almost three days and I thought maybe I was dreaming. Maybe I am dreaming.

---

* The year can be modified to the year of performance. "Yaaasss" could be exchanged with any current exlcaimable catch phrase of approval. i.e. "yolo," "totes," etc.

ELLIE. Is he a leprechaun?

JAMIE. Donna thought he was the sublet –

DONNA. Whose name is 'Chaz,' by the way.

ELLIE. Chaz? Ew, what?

DONNA. Right?

JAMIE. Bitches! Who is that guy?

DONNA. Shh! You're going to wake him up.

(DONNA *quietly shuts door #3.*)

JAMIE. I'm not worried about that random dude getting a great night's sleep. I'm worried about me getting any sleep at all ever.

DONNA. I know. So let's stop for a minute, figure out who he is and get him out of here. He came from over there.

ELLIE. He wasn't in my room when I went to bed –

JAMIE. He wasn't in mine until just now –

DONNA. He wasn't in mine when I went to change –

ELLIE. Got it!

JAMIE. What?

DONNA. What?

ELLIE. Wait? Nevermind.

DONNA. OOH!

JAMIE. What?

DONNA. Nope.

ELLIE. WAIT!

JAMIE. What?

DONNA. What?

ELLIE. Got it!

JAMIE. What?

ELLIE. Are you sure it's not Chaz?

JAMIE. YES!

ELLIE. When does Chaz get here?

JAMIE. The day after tomorrow.

ELLIE. He could be early.

JAMIE. That's not Chaz.

ELLIE. You don't know. You've never met the guy.

JAMIE. I've known him for years.

ELLIE. Oh.

JAMIE. That is not Chaz.

ELLIE. Oh.

DONNA. That's right! Chaz is the one from London.

ELLIE. Chaz is the one from London!

DONNA. He said the thing. What was it that he said?

JAMIE. What?

ELLIE. The funny thing –

DONNA. He said something funny when you two hooked up. What did he say?

ELLIE. Something funny like "awesome member."

DONNA. No not "awesome member."

ELLIE. Right, no. "Huge wang, mate."

DONNA. What was it? Tip of my tongue.

ELLIE. Yes! I know it. It was "Great Co –

JAMIE. Stop.

DONNA. Yes yes yes – "Great Co –

JAMIE. Stop! Don't say it.

DONNA. Why not? So good. "Great Co –

JAMIE. NO!

DONNA. Giving a sensible handy and then he pauses and is like "Great co –

JAMIE. NO. Bad Donna.

ELLIE. All British and sexual. I like Chaz already. He'll be a fun roomie.

JAMIE. Drop it, Ellie.

ELLIE. Jamie, you maneater you. It's like first Chaz and now Theo. Meow.

JAMIE. What is wrong with you?

ELLIE. What?

DONNA. She did St. Patty's Day.

ELLIE. I'm an adult. I've had an adult beverage or eight.

DONNA. So did Theo.

JAMIE. Theo what?

DONNA. He did St. Patty's – not the soberest.

JAMIE. No I never would have guessed.

DONNA. Don't be snarky.

JAMIE. Who is Theo, Donna?

DONNA. I don't know, Jamie.

JAMIE. How did he get in my room?

DONNA. I put him there.

JAMIE. Why?

DONNA. Because he was your sublet.

ELLIE. I thought that was Chaz.

JAMIE. It is.

ELLIE. Chaz and Theo? Are they together?

DONNA. No.

ELLIE. But they're sharing the room?

JAMIE. No.

ELLIE. I wish we still had the bunk beds.

JAMIE. I wish I knew who the man in my bed was.

DONNA. Been there.

ELLIE. Ditto. Ooh! If Theo really was a leprechaun, he could grant all of our wishes.

DONNA. That would be nice. I'd make a new wish though.

ELLIE. I want a puppy.

JAMIE. This is stupid. I'm waking him and kicking him out.

DONNA. Wait, Jamie.

JAMIE. Oh my god.

DONNA. What?

ELLIE. Oh my god.

DONNA. What? What? I can't see around you.

ELLIE. He's not in the bed anymore.

DONNA. Where is he? Where did he go?

> (JAMIE, ELLIE *and* DONNA *stand at door #3 and look for* THEO.)

Where did he go?

ELLIE. I don't know.

> (THEO *comes bumbling out of door #1 as quietly as possible. No one sees him as he sneaks up behind the group.*)

JAMIE. You shouldn't have shut the door.

ELLIE. He could be waiting under the bed to cut your Achilles. I heard people do that. Under cars and stuff.

JAMIE. That's scary.

THEO. Hey.

ELLIE. AHHH!

DONNA. AHH!

JAMIE. AGHWHAT?

THEO. AHHH!

DONNA. Theo!

ELLIE. Theo!

DONNA. How did you get out here?

JAMIE. That's him! That's the man from my bed!

ELLIE. Theo.

THEO. RAWR!!

JAMIE. What? What? What is that?

THEO. GRAWWWR!!

JAMIE. Is he pretending to be a dinosaur?

THEO. I'm an herbivore.

DONNA. Theo is *really* wasted, by the way.

THEO. I was waiting to go to the bathroom and someone asked me "coke?" and I was like "Noke" but then I got the coke in my face anyway but I didn't mean to. It was an accident but they meant to give it to me in my nose.

ELLIE. You poor baby.

THEO. Rawr!

ELLIE. Rawr!

DONNA. —

JAMIE. —

ELLIE. Hi, Theo. I'm Ellie.

THEO. I'm a The-saurus.

ELLIE. Rawr! So how do you know Jamie?

JAMIE. Stop rawr-ing. How'd you get in here?

THEO. Raw –

DONNA. Theodore!

THEO. Sorry.

ELLIE. He's hysterical. Leprechaun and a dinosaur.

THEO. Lepre-saurus. "Top of the mawwwwrrrrnin' to ya!"

ELLIE. I like your outfit.

THEO. I like yours.

ELLIE. Irish twinsies. I love him. Where did this guy come from?

DONNA. Shut up. You're not Irish. Either of you.

ELLIE. But my great-great grandparents –

THEO. I'm one thirty second –

ELLIE. And I have a claddagh ring!

DONNA. Exactly. You're American. I'm American. It's fine.

JAMIE. Donna, focus. These two are useless. Help me. When did he come in?

DONNA. Right after she went to bed.

ELLIE. I'm American but my ethnicity is Irish.

DONNA. That's a nationality not an ethnicity.

JAMIE. He came through the front door?

DONNA. He didn't come in the front door.

THEO. Are you sure?

DONNA. Are you sure?

THEO. No.

JAMIE. Where was he when you found him?

DONNA. I was on the couch reading and I heard the bedroom door open and thought it was Ellie –

ELLIE. Was it me?

DONNA. No, Ellie. It was Theo.

ELLIE. That's fair.

JAMIE. And you didn't ask where he came from? Of course not.

DONNA. I thought he was Chaz. What is that supposed to mean?

ELLIE. Are Theo and Chaz similar looking?

DONNA. I've never met him.

JAMIE. Not at all. It means go figure. I'm not surprised.

ELLIE. Why'd you think Theo was Chaz?

DONNA. I thought Theo was the sublet. Surprised about what?

ELLIE. I don't get it.

DONNA. I thought Theo was the sublet so I walked him to his room and shut the door.

JAMIE. His room which is my room that I was still in which you should have known.

THEO. I took a nap. What did you do?

DONNA. My door was open so I shut it. Sorry if I forgot what day you were leaving. I've got a lot on my plate.

JAMIE. You shut your door and then what? And you don't have a lot on your plate. You go to the office and come home. That's it.

DONNA. And I went to the fridge and then – and then – I do not. Why are you even saying that?

JAMIE. You got us into this.

DONNA. Theo is just mysteriously here and that's my fault?

ELLIE. It is mysterious. How did he get here?

DONNA. I don't know.

JAMIE. Some random guy is in our apartment and you just make friends with him without a doubt or question.

DONNA. I thought he was Chaz. I put him in your room and you came out yelling. I don't know.

JAMIE. Theo, how did you get in here?

THEO. It's a very nice apartment.

ELLIE. Thank you.

JAMIE. Useless.

THEO. Very cozy.

ELLIE. Thank you! I was just at Ikea a few days ago and I spent like 180 dollars on stuff to make it homey. Too much, I know. Did you know we didn't have a wine rack? A wine wrack! So I bought one.

JAMIE. Look, I don't even care any more. Theo, you have to leave now. It is the middle of the night and I'm getting pissed.

THEO. Why?

ELLIE. We call him the dragon when he's tired.

JAMIE. You don't live here and we do.

THEO. I'll just stay in room.

ELLIE. Like 'don't wake the dragon.' Hilarious.

DONNA. Theo, that is my room.

THEO. Slumber party.

ELLIE. I really miss the bunk beds.

THEO. Did you know we like each other. Donnie thinks I'm handsome.

DONNA. Donna. And don't start. He told me that he was handsome. It wasn't really my idea.

ELLIE. Theo, I think you are very handsome.

THEO. Other girl, I'm sorry. I love Donnie.

DONNA. Donna.

THEO. I know. Shh.

JAMIE. Love? Seriously? Time to go Theo! Time to go.

THEO. I don't wanna.

JAMIE. Sorry but I'm over this. Don't forget to write. You need to go or I'm going to call the cops.

ELLIE. Don't be stupid, Jamie. Just because he likes Donnie and not you –

DONNA. Donna.

JAMIE. I don't give two shits about who he likes. He broke into our house. Are y'all stupid or something?

THEO. Don't call them stupid.

JAMIE. Shut up and get out of my apartment.

THEO. Stop yelling at me.

JAMIE. Stop standing in my apartment.

THEO. I can't fly.

ELLIE. Got you there.

JAMIE. Really? Because you're high as a kite. I'm calling the cops.

DONNA. Hold on. Theo, I'm sorry but you've got to go home now. Jamie is getting pissed and when he is sleepy and grumpy and snarky he goes to a place. He starts blaming people for things that they shouldn't be blamed for and it is not a good scene.

JAMIE. Donna, someone needs to take responsibility for this ridiculousness. You should have called the cops right away.

DONNA. I practically screamed bloody murder when he first came in. So maybe it's your fault for not being in tune with my distress.

JAMIE. You're always in distress. You hoot like that every day.

DONNA. Ooh! I do not hoot. Whatever. Theo, you need to go.

THEO. I'm not scared of this twirp.

JAMIE. Twirp? Are you out of your mind? I will ruin your life you pretty-faced son of a bitch.

ELLIE. Oh my.

THEO. Gimme yer shot.

JAMIE. Gimme yer shot? Oh, I'll give you my shot.—Get this wasted asshole out of my house!

ELLIE. Alright, Theo –

DONNA. Goodnight, Theo.

THEO. Fuck you, Theo!

ELLIE. Everyone knock it off with the potty mouth!

> (**THEO** *goes back into dinosaur mode and charges around the apartment. He knocks things over and makes an absolute scene.*)

JAMIE. —

Seriously? Go home.

THEO. You go home.

JAMIE. You go home.

THEO. Go home.

JAMIE. You go home.

THEO. You go home.

JAMIE. Go home.

THEO. You go home.

JAMIE. You go home right now!

THEO. You!

JAMIE. NO.

THEO. Go home.

JAMIE. NO!

ELLIE. Jamie.

JAMIE. No. I will not go home. This guy can't tell me what to do in my own house. I will not go home. I don't want to go home!

THEO. Dude.

ELLIE. Jamie.

JAMIE. What?

ELLIE. You are home.

THEO. Go home!

JAMIE. Shut up!

> (**JAMIE** *lunges at* **THEO** *but* **THEO** *sprints into door #2 and locks himself inside.*)

ELLIE. He's in my room!

JAMIE. That's what he does. He goes in rooms. Open this door right now!

DONNA. Theo! Theo, it's Donn-ie. Please open the door.

ELLIE. Donna.

DONNA. Please open the door.

JAMIE. Open up! This is the police!

ELLIE. It's not really, that's Jamie.

JAMIE. Shut up, Ellie.

DONNA. Theo, please open the door. You're really wasted and I'm worried.

> (Once again, **THEO** quietly and calmly opens door #1 and enters the living room. No one sees him.)

ELLIE. Theo, if you come out I'll make you hot chocolate! Or a beer. You want a beersie?

JAMIE. Ellie, stop.

ELLIE. Rawr! Does The-saurus want a salad?

JAMIE. Stop offering him stuff.

DONNA. Stop scolding her.

ELLIE. I'm baiting him to lure him out.

JAMIE. That's not going to work.

ELLIE. Well I don't see you succeeding.

DONNA. I'm getting worried, Theo. Please just let us know you're okay.

Theo?

ELLIE. He probably fell asleep.

JAMIE. Passed out.

ELLIE. He could have hit his head. He could be bleeding.

JAMIE. He's drunk. He's going to piss the bed.

ELLIE. I just got new sheets. I just got new sheets. I just got new sheets!

Theo, do not piss that bed!

JAMIE. He's probably dead. OD'd on Ellie's duvet.

THEO. Dude, I'm fine.

ELLIE. BAH!

DONNA. OH MY GOD.

JAMIE. Oh. Oh. Oh! I'm done with this.

(JAMIE *takes out his phone.*)

ELLIE. How do you keep doing that?

DONNA. But you were in there –

ELLIE. That was awesome. Totally magical!

JAMIE. Hi! I'd like to report a break in.

DONNA. And then you were there. There then there.

ELLIE. Wait. Don't, Jamie.

DONNA. What are you doing? What is that? Stop it.

JAMIE. I am talking to the cops and we are finishing this mess.

ELLIE. Don't call the cops.

JAMIE. Yeah, he's actually still inside. Sitting on my couch.

(JAMIE *goes into door #3.* THEO *gets out his phone and also calls the police.*)

THEO. You can't arrest me. D'you know who I am?

DONNA. No, actually, we don't. We don't know you at all.

ELLIE. Who are you?

THEO. Donnie you know me.

DONNA. No I don't. Theo, you are probably great but you're wasted and you've got to get out of here.

THEO. I don't want to leave you. Hello? I'd like to report a butthead.

ELLIE. He means Jamie.

DONNA. I know. No, Theo, No. Give me the phone.

THEO. Number six at 30–17 23rd Ave. He's a total butthead and he's mad at me for chatting up this pretty damsel.

ELLIE. He really likes you!

DONNA. I don't even know this guy. And I am not a damsel. Theo, it's time to go.

(DONNA *grabs the phone.*)

DONNA. Thank you. I'm so sorry our friends are just drunk. And stupid. Yes, sorry, it's actually apartment four but everything is fine. I'm sober and dealing. So sorry. Happy St. Patty's Day.

(**DONNA** *hangs up the phone.*)

DONNA. The police are probably going to come anyway.

THEO. The only rule when I was tiny was that I shouldn't get myself into any trouble that I couldn't get myself out of.

ELLIE. Good rule.

DONNA. That's really cute.

THEO. You think I'm so cute.

DONNA. You are cute but you just have to go, I'm sorry.

THEO. I'll marry you.

(**THEO** *gets on one knee.*)

ELLIE. Aww!

THEO. Donnie Marie Ascot, would you marry me?

DONNA. That's not my name, actually, and – It's very sweet of you to ask but I just don't think that I am ready –

(**JAMIE** *comes out of the bedroom.*)

JAMIE. The cops are on their way so pack up your stuff and get – what in the world is going on?

ELLIE. It was so cute. Theo proposed and Donna legit looked like she wanted to say yes –

DONNA. Not uh –

ELLIE. – but then she didn't, obviously, and it was really cute. He got down on one knee and said "Donnie Marie Ascot, would you marry me?"

JAMIE. That's not her name.

THEO. Exactly.

JAMIE. What?

THEO. You know her name and I don't even.

JAMIE. You're an idiot.

THEO. I'm a Leprechaun.

JAMIE. And a dinosaur and a drug addict and I'm really over this.

(**JAMIE** *starts to physically push* **THEO** *out the door.*)

JAMIE. Get out of my house now!

> (THEO *puts up a bit of a fight and the boys begin to grapple. Neither of them knows how to fight; they look ridiculous.*)

DONNA. Stop it!

ELLIE. You two are so dumb. Stop it. Stop. You're going to hit the wine rack!

> (JAMIE *hits* THEO *in the face.*)

JAMIE. That's right! Ouch. Shit. Yeah, bitch!

> (THEO *is on the ground motionless.*)

ELLIE. Oh god. He's dead. You killed him.

DONNA. He's not dead. He's wasted.

JAMIE. And I knocked his ass out.

ELLIE. He isn't moving. I think you killed him.

JAMIE. He's not dead.

DONNA. What the hell, Jamie?

> (JAMIE *grabs* THEO *by the arms and drags him out the front door.*)

DONNA. Stop it! Just let him be. He isn't hurting anyone.

ELLIE. *(beginning to cry)* Because he is dead. Donna, you promised!

> (*He comes back inside and locks the door.*)

JAMIE. And that is how we do it.

DONNA. You just punched that guy for no reason.

JAMIE. He was trying to fight me.

DONNA. You were pushing him.

ELLIE. He could be bleeding internally.

JAMIE. That guy broke into our apartment and was basically assaulting you, Donna.

DONNA. He was not.

JAMIE. He was hitting on you. He was getting handsy.

DONNA. So?

ELLIE. He probably has a subdural hematoma.

JAMIE. So? He was wasted. What would have happened if he tried to make a move on you and we weren't here? Who knows how far he would have tried to take things.

ELLIE. He needs a CT.

DONNA. And what if he had, Jamie?

JAMIE. What?

DONNA. I'm a grown-ass woman. I can handle a guy hitting on me. Not like it's the first time.

(**ELLIE** *gets out her phone.*)

JAMIE. It's not getting a catcall. He broke into our house somehow. Plus – You have a boyfriend.

DONNA. Only sort of. And that means Theo isn't allowed to think I'm beautiful? He thinks I am beautiful.

ELLIE. Hello? I think my friend just killed a guy.

JAMIE. What? No I didn't, Ellie.

DONNA. That he isn't allowed to give me attention? I think I'm entitled to a little bit of something, Jamie.

ELLIE. Punched him straight in the head.

JAMIE. Hang up the phone – you're going to get me arrested.

DONNA. He's a nice and successful guy and I don't see why I should have to shy away from someone like that. He's a good person.

JAMIE. You don't know that.

DONNA. Yes, I do.

JAMIE. How? How could you possibly?

DONNA. Sometimes you can just tell if people are good.

JAMIE. That doesn't make any sense.

ELLIE. I can't check – he's in the hallway. 30–17 23rd Avenue apartment four.

DONNA. Exactly my point.

ELLIE. Please hurry. I'm so afraid.

JAMIE. I'm not a good person? I'm a miraculous person. Don't turn this around on me.

DONNA. I think you are the one who turned this around on me actually.

> (**THEO** *begins to make noise outside the door. He knocks on the door.*)

THEO. Huh'llo?

ELLIE. He's alive!

> (**ELLIE** *hangs up her phone.*)

Hello? Theo? Oh my god. Theo, are you alive?

THEO. Ouchies.

ELLIE. I need you to let me know if you're alive.

THEO. Open the door please.

JAMIE. Eleanor don't you dare. Addict, this isn't your apartment. Now tell the cops he's not dead before I'm incarcerated.

ELLIE. I can't.

JAMIE. Why not?

ELLIE. I hung up. Theo, are you okay?

THEO. —

ELLIE. Theo? Theo?

DONNA. Ellie you can't hang up on the police. It just makes things worse.

> (**DONNA** *picks up the phone and calls the police.*)

ELLIE. Clap twice if you're dead.

DONNA. Hi there. Just calling again about apartment four at 23rd ave.

ELLIE. I'm going to check on him.

> (**ELLIE** *unlocks the door and opens it.* **THEO** *is passed out in the doorway.*)

JAMIE. Ellie, shut the door. He's fine.

> (**JAMIE** *slams the door shut.*)

ELLIE. He is not fine, Jameson.

JAMIE. Not my name.

DONNA. Everything is fine. No one is dead. I hope. My friends are just drunk and – Hello? Hello?

ELLIE. He is probably bleeding or seizing and, if he isn't already deceased, he is going to wake up in a coma.

DONNA. She hung up on me.

(*ELLIE opens the door again.*)

JAMIE. Stop it, Ellie!

ELLIE. I'm worried.

JAMIE. We're the victims of a home invasion and you're both acting like it's nothing.

DONNA. Can cops do that? Can cops hang up on you?

JAMIE. He's lucky I didn't actually kill him.

ELLIE. What if you did? What if you killed him and now we have to hide the body. A twist in the plot.

JAMIE. Why would we do that?

(*JAMIE slams the door. THEO is still outside.*)

ELLIE. Just let me check his pulse. The old one, two pulse pulse checky.

DONNA. She's getting a piece of my tongue.

(*DONNA calls the police again.*)

JAMIE. They can check.

ELLIE. And if he's with the Lord by the time they get here? I will not have that blood on my hands.

(*ELLIE opens the door. THEO has disappeared.*)

JAMIE. There is no blood. Ellie stop it or I'm going to kill you too.

(*JAMIE slams the door. Then opens the door again. THEO is missing. JAMIE shuts the door.*)

DONNA. Hi! Oh. Hi, I was just calling because I was calling before about apartment four at 30–17 23rd Ave and, though I don't want assume that it was deliberate, I think I was hung up on by one of your dispatchers.

JAMIE. He's not dead.

ELLIE. What if he was undead? Let's go with that.

DONNA. No, ma'am, I think it was you, MA'AM. Now, ma'am, everything is fine I just wanted to check –

ELLIE. And on the fateful night, our delicate hero Jameson single-handedly caused the beginning of the Zombie Apocalypse. Donna!

DONNA. Shh! Wait. I just want to check back in –

ELLIE. Donna.

DONNA. Check back in and let you know that –

ELLIE. Donna!

DONNA. Seriously, Ellie? What?

ELLIE. Theo disappeared.

DONNA. What?

ELLIE. He's a zombie now.

*(**DONNA** hangs up the phone again.)*

DONNA. Where did he go?

JAMIE. Who cares? Stupid wasted leprechaun.

DONNA. That wasted leprechaun was kind of wonderful.

ELLIE. May he rest in peace.

JAMIE. He's not dead.

DONNA. You don't get it.

ELLIE. You don't know that.

JAMIE. Am I on paint or something? How are you into this guy?

DONNA. I don't see how you don't see it.

JAMIE. You're being such an idiot.

DONNA. At least I'm not the one assaulting people. How's the knuckle, butthead?

JAMIE. Feels pretty fabulous, mother fu –

ELLIE. Alright knock it off!

JAMIE. —

DONNA. —

ELLIE. In this dark hour, I'd like to take a moment and have a conversation about our feelings.

JAMIE. Ellie, I haven't slept in days and one of the biggest days of my career is set to start in like three hours –

DONNA. I'm jittery and I just don't wannnnnnnna –

ELLIE. When we express ourselves like children we are treated like children.

> (ELLIE *retrieves a talking stick.*)

JAMIE. Oh god.

ELLIE. Jamie, why don't you begin.

> (ELLIE *hands* JAMIE *the talking stick. The rules of the talking stick are understood between them. Only the person holding the stick can speak.*)

JAMIE. Fine. I'm upset because she could have gotten us killed with her googly feelings about that lepresaurus-douche.

DONNA. I'm upset because it was an honest mistake and I'm being blamed. It's not like I knew he was a stranger. I thought he was Chaz.

ELLIE. Chaz from London. Not yet arrived.

DONNA. Nothing bad happened. Except for the fact that Theo is going to wake up with a black eye and a serious hangover.

JAMIE. Exactly. He probably isn't going to remember any of this or you and you're practically picking out colors for the nursery.

DONNA. Can you blame me? Theo might have been wasted but he's successful and hot and gives great advice.

And at least he believes in me. We talked and I think I'm going to quit my job. Leap into the net. Force myself to actually do what I want to do.

JAMIE. Whoa. Let's slow the plow for a moment shall we.

DONNA. And you know what? I think he will remember tonight. We're connected. He understands me and tomorrow morning we're going to hydrate and prove you wrong.

JAMIE. You've gone totally bat-shit.

DONNA. Maybe! But at least I'm going to be happy. I am smart and talented and beautiful.

JAMIE. No one is denying that.

DONNA. I want to be the exceptional one who succeeds young and gets to do what I was trained to do.

JAMIE. You're seriously going to base a huge decision like this on the advice you got from a total stranger that broke into our apartment in the middle of the night high on coke, drunk out of his mind and dressed as a leprechaun?

DONNA. Of course it sounds bad when you say it like that.

JAMIE. That is exactly how it was.

DONNA. I'm still quitting. And it really isn't about him or because of him. This is for me.

JAMIE. And what about Matt?

ELLIE. Matt. Unseen boyfriend of questionable importance.

JAMIE. Just going to quit him too?

DONNA. Yup. Clean sweep. Matt isn't even a name. It's a thing you put in front of your door. Theo has a face like a big puppy dog, Jamie. You know I love that.

JAMIE. Yeah but who doesn't love puppies?

ELLIE. Zombies.

DONNA. Please just try and put yourself in my socks. I am so sick of settling. This feels good and I want something different.

(**DONNA** *gets out her phone and starts a call.*)

JAMIE. I've worn the socks, Donna. Tore holes in the heels.

DONNA. Jamie, I just feel it.

JAMIE. Who are you calling?

DONNA. Cruella.

JAMIE. No. Wait. What? Donna, stop! Alright. Okay. Fine. Let's – let's talk more about Theo. So cute, right? Hang up the phone. It's the middle of the night.

DONNA. Carpe Noche, bitches. Voicemail.

Hi! Hello, Marjory. Can I call you Marjory? I know you typically prefer something more formal but we know each other pretty well, I think, and I'd say it's time we had a little talk about my current position of employment.

JAMIE. Ask for a promotion. Ask for a raise.

DONNA. If you could call me back at 646-297 — Eh. Nevermind. I quit. Because I am a net and you can leap into me. That's not right. The point is I quit! Booyah!

—

Thank you for the opportunity. That's all. Bye.

JAMIE. You're out of your mind.

(There is a knock on the front door.)

DONNA. Oh thank god! Theo, I did it!

*(**DONNA** opens the door. **OFFICER PERKINS** stands on the other side.)*

OFFICER PERKINS. Hello.

DONNA. Hi.

OFFICER PERKINS. May I come in?

DONNA. Um.

*(**DONNA** slams the door in **PERKINS**' face.)*

(blackout)

End of Act I

ACT II

(That same night. That same moment.)

DONNA. Oh my god.

OFFICER PERKINS. *(offstage)* You shut the door.

JAMIE. Donna, open the door.

ELLIE. Don't open the door.

DONNA. Sorry!

JAMIE. Open the door.

ELLIE. No. Shut it.

DONNA. It is shut.

OFFICER PERKINS. *(offstage)* I'm a police officer.

ELLIE. Don't open it.

OFFICER PERKINS. *(offstage)* We received several calls – five calls – about a disturbance at this address.

ELLIE. If we don't move they won't be able to see us.

DONNA. This isn't Jurassic Park. He knows we're here.

POLICE. *(offstage)* A break in, a murder, hang-ups, and a butthead.

ELLIE. Don't open the door. I can't go down like this.

DONNA. Oh my god. He's going to take Theo away. We have to save Theo.

OFFICER PERKINS. *(offstage)* I can hear you whispering.

ELLIE. We have the right to remain quiet.

JAMIE. I'm opening the door –

ELLIE & DONNA. DON'T!

JAMIE. We're ending these shenanigans.

DONNA. Jamie, no! You're going to get Theo arrested.

JAMIE. If I'm lucky.

(JAMIE *opens the front door.* **OFFICER PERKINS,**
who is awkward and nervous, does not enter.)

OFFICER PERKINS. Thank you.

ELLIE. I'm not going down without a fight.

OFFICER PERKINS. Who is fighting? I'm an officer of the
law.

DONNA. Ellie, you didn't do anything. Stop it.

OFFICER PERKINS. What did not you do? Explain.

JAMIE. Yes, officer, we will.

ELLIE. Donna, I'd like you to be my attorney.

DONNA. Not the time, El.

ELLIE. I won't speak until my lawyer is present.

JAMIE. Officer you can come inside.

OFFICER PERKINS. Oh. Are you sure? Thank you. Yes. I'll
just come in then.

JAMIE. Can we get you anything? Water, coffee?

DONNA. I'll take a cup of coffee.

OFFICER PERKINS. I'd like to get to work. I'd like to know
what am I doing here tonight? And some water.

(JAMIE *makes the water and coffee.*)

DONNA. Officer, it's a long complicated story but I promise
that everything is fine. You can actually head back out.

OFFICER PERKINS. Oh, you're fine? Everything is fine.

DONNA. Everything is great.

OFFICER PERKINS. Thank goodness. That was easy. Nailed
it. I'll just go then, goodnight –

JAMIE. A man broke into our apartment earlier.

DONNA. No one broke in. I don't know what he's talking
about.

OFFICER PERKINS. Which is it?

DONNA. We're fine.

JAMIE. A man broke into the apartment but then he
disappeared.

OFFICER PERKINS. When was this? More water please.

JAMIE. Earlier tonight. Are you okay?

OFFICER PERKINS. Sure I'm fine. Why? Do I not seem fine? I'm very assertive and poised. Who is the man?

DONNA. Who?

JAMIE. You seem nervous. You're shaking. We don't know.

OFFICER PERKINS. Don't know what?

JAMIE. Who the man is.

OFFICER PERKINS. I'm not nervous. I'm a strong officer of peacekeeping. I don't have nerves. I'm winded. Three flights of stairs. How did he break into your apartment?

DONNA. He didn't.

JAMIE. He was in the apartment but we don't know how he got in.

DONNA. I don't know what you're talking about. Ellie, back me up.

ELLIE. —

DONNA. Ellie, help me out. There was no one here, right?

JAMIE. Tell him the truth, Ellie.

DONNA. I'll be your lawyer. You're my first client.

ELLIE. Score. Yeah. No. I don't – No one was even here I think. What? What are you even – what? I don't know.

JAMIE. I'm going to kill you.

OFFICER PERKINS. Threat! Threat on the scene. Is that a threat?

JAMIE. It's a figure of speech.

ELLIE. And a terrifying reality.

JAMIE. Do not. Do not do this, Ellie.

OFFICER PERKINS. Young Man –

JAMIE. I'm thirty-two.

OFFICER PERKINS. Kid, do not test me tonight. Not tonight.

JAMIE. I'm not testing –

OFFICER PERKINS. Was there an intruder here tonight or not?

JAMIE. Yes

DONNA. NO

ELLIE. Yee-OO

OFFICER PERKINS. Did a man break into this apartment tonight?

JAMIE. Yes – Yes he did –

DONNA. No – He didn't –

ELLIE. What? – Who?

DONNA. No, Officer.

JAMIE. Yes, Officer.

DONNA. No.

JAMIE. Yes.

DONNA. Jamie!

JAMIE. Donna!

ELLIE. Ellie!

OFFICER PERKINS. HEY. Knock it off. There is a lot going on here. I need to be less confused. This could be a big case. I'm sweating. I need more information. Big. Real big. Talk.

DONNA. Okay.

OFFICER PERKINS. And water. More water.

DONNA. Officer, it's the silliest thing. My friend Ellie here –

ELLIE. But call me Ellie.

DONNA. She was out celebrating for St. Patrick's Day and, when she came home, she and I got into a semi-loud conversation. Ellie's voice must have sounded a bit husky. I guess Jamie thought he heard a man's voice but it was just Ellie.

OFFICER PERKINS. Why did you call 911 so many times? That's excessive. Nerve-wracking.

DONNA. I didn't –

OFFICER PERKINS. Then who did?

JAMIE. I called to report –

ELLIE. I called once because he –

DONNA. I called twice after they hung –

OFFICER PERKINS. That's four.

JAMIE. Theo called once.

OFFICER PERKINS. Who is Theo?

ELLIE. What? Who? Who is that? Theo? An mysterious fifth player in a game of he-said-she-said?

JAMIE. Theo is the guy who broke in.

DONNA. No he didn't.

JAMIE. I called first because he broke in but wouldn't leave.

OFFICER PERKINS. Who called next?

DONNA. Ellie did in her pretend man voice. To play a joke on Jamie.

ELLIE. *(In her 'husky' voice)* I'm calling to report a big old stinky butthead, bro.

JAMIE. Ellie, drop it.

DONNA. Officer, I'm a lawyer –

JAMIE. Sort of –

DONNA. – So I know the law and everything here is fine.

JAMIE. She doesn't work in criminal law and she just quit her job via voicemail.

DONNA. I'm between positions.

ELLIE. She will be acting as my representation.

JAMIE. Ellie, she can't represent you.

ELLIE. Why not?

JAMIE. She's not that kind of lawyer.

ELLIE. Oh my.

JAMIE. So you better stop playing one of your little games before you really get in trouble.

ELLIE. Oh my. Thank you Jamie for showing me the light. I will tell the truth.

DONNA. Wait –

ELLIE. Your honor, Theo is real.

DONNA. Who is Theo? What?

ELLIE. I didn't make that husky voiced call. He called and then Jamie called then and I called after Jamie killed Theo.

DONNA. Ellie hung up on the dispatchers during that call so I called to let them know that Theo was fine.

OFFICER PERKINS. Is the intruder real?

ELLIE. He is. Jamie killed him.

JAMIE. Ellie, I did not kill him. I punched him. He ran off somewhere.

OFFICER PERKINS. Ma'am I need you to be very straight with me right now. I can't take statements like that lightly. Is it hot in here? It's really hot.

JAMIE. Tell him Theo's not dead.

ELLIE. I took an oath, Jamie.

JAMIE. No you didn't.

DONNA. He disappeared after Jamie hit him.

OFFICER PERKINS. I thought Theo wasn't real in your story.

DONNA. Well – maybe he is and if Theo was real and had been allegedly knocked out and the police had been allegedly called –

OFFICER PERKINS. They were. I'm sure of it. This is a lot. It's so hot.

DONNA. If they were, Ellie would have allegedly hung up on 911 when she thought he allegedly was dead so I allegedly called back to let them know we were all fine but I was hung up on. I called that friggin' lady back to express my dissatisfaction with her service.

JAMIE. More to the point, I didn't kill anyone.

OFFICER PERKINS. Stand back, perp!

DONNA. Then I hung up on her when Theo disappeared.

ELLIE. Jamie, this is the story and I was born to tell it. I can't stop now, just roll with me on this. You punched him out and now he's about dead as a doornail.

JAMIE. Pay no attention to her. She's loves embellishing. He obviously didn't die –

ELLIE. Right. What do I know? I'm just the one who has seen every episode of *E.R.*, *Grey's Anatomy*, *General Hospital* and *I Love Lucy* so I guess I know absolutely nothing about medicine.

DONNA. Those shows are notoriously inaccurate in –

ELLIE. Theo's battered and bloody body disappeared. Officer Anxious, he has come back from the dead.

OFFICER PERKINS. I'm sorry?

JAMIE. I brought him into the hallway for you to take care of and locked him out. Ellie went to check on him and he was gone. He's not –

ELLIE. My expertise leads me to know that he is a Zombie. Or a Vampire. Or, let's be honest, we might be dealing with Jesus herself for all I know.

OFFICER PERKINS. Now we're all going to die?

DONNA. No one is going to die.

OFFICER PERKINS. This is my first night in uniform. I cannot be the rookie that shows up on a routine drunk call and winds up having my face eaten off. This is why I moved out of Florida in the first place.

JAMIE. Officer, your face is not going to be eaten.

OFFICER PERKINS. I'm so hot.

JAMIE. We just need you to find the Theo and arrest him.

ELLIE. Theo is the zombie –

JAMIE. The intruder –

OFFICER PERKINS. You want me to arrest a Zombie? I'm getting out of here.

> (**THEO** *re-enters through door #1. No one sees him but* **DONNA.** *She remains quiet and motions for* **THEO** *to stay quiet as well. She sneaks away and brings* **THEO** *back out door #1.*)

ELLIE. He could be right outside! If you stick with me and listen to everything I have to say, we can survive this thing but we're going to need to work as a team.

JAMIE. We're not playing games right now.

OFFICER PERKINS. Kid, I'm gonna be honest with you. I'm not listening to you. I think we need to let this woman lead the way to safety.

ELLIE. We are in mortal danger.

(**DONNA** *comes out of door #1 alone and shuts the door behind her and gets a cup of coffee.*)

JAMIE. This officer is working, Ellie. Stop playing. You need to get sober and edit, I've got to catch a bus, Donna obviously needs to see a psychiatrist –

OFFICER PERKINS. I want to hear what the shaky girl has to say.

DONNA. Me?

JAMIE. You've got to be kidding me.

ELLIE. Ooh coffee. I want a drink.

(**ELLIE** *gets a beer.*)

OFFICER PERKINS. Don't mock me. I'm the one with the uniform and the badge so I can make the call about who speaks. I'm a cop.

JAMIE. Then do your job and find the guy who broke into my damn apartment.

OFFICER PERKINS. Do my job? Did you just tell me to do my job?

JAMIE. Yes. I did. Please do your job and leave. I am strung out on exhaustion and all I want to do is go to bed.

DONNA. Have some of my coffee it helps with the sleep thing.

OFFICER PERKINS. You kids these days have no respect for authority.

JAMIE. I am thirty-two years old.

OFFICER PERKINS. I'm a professional keeper of the peace. I'm a strong, confident protector of justice with a baby on the way.

ELLIE & DONNA. Congratulations!

OFFICER PERKINS. It was an accident – but I'll be damned if I'm going to go down because of a vampire and some whiny kids on St. Patrick's Day before that little nugget is born.

JAMIE. I'm going to jump off the balcony.

DONNA. Please don't. The neighbors will leave another passive aggressive note in the lobby when they have to clean up your guts.

JAMIE. I just want to go to sleep.

ELLIE. But the guts might be the perfect way to lure Theo back. (So do it.)

OFFICER. This just got real, young man, so I'm going to need you to buck up and get on board or I will have to detain you until we have things under control. Be a part of the team.

ELLIE. Be a part of the team, Jamie.

OFFICER PERKINS. Be on the team or off the team.

ELLIE. On or off.

OFFICER PERKINS. You on the team? I'll cuff you to the table. You on?

ELLIE. Come on, Jamie. You on the team?

JAMIE. No! Absolutely not. I'm not playing into this mess. Officer, please take a breath –

OFFICER PERKINS. You leave me no choice.

JAMIE. Get away from me!

OFFICER PERKINS. If you will not comply with the request of an officer then you will be detained against your will.

JAMIE. You're not making Donna get on the team.

OFFICER PERKINS. I have overlooked the fact that you are being accused of murder because the victim of this attack has risen from the grave and apparently seeks vengeance. Give me your arm. I have to detain you.

JAMIE. I don't believe this. It's like five in the morning and I haven't slept in three days preparing for what could literally be a make-it-or-break-it deal for my entire career. What should I be doing? Sleeping. Resting. "Resting is an action," that's what you always say, Ellie.

ELLIE. I do say that.

JAMIE. And what am I doing? I'm losing my mind as some crazy stranger runs around my building making my best friends act like lunatics and I am so tired. Ellie, stop saying I killed him. He is not dead. I just want to go to bed. I want to snuggle up with Wilson –

ELLIE. That's his stuffed penguin –

JAMIE. And finally sleep. What did I do to deserve this?

OFFICER PERKINS. You can whine and victimize yourself all you want kid, but this is real life and we're not going to stop until this situation has been contained. You've got three seconds before I arrest you and pop you in the back of my car. One, two, –

JAMIE. Fine fine fine. Arrest me!

OFFICER PERKINS. Here we go. Turn around and face the wall.

>(OFFICER PERKINS *proceeds to clumsily detain* JAMIE *but is unable to work the cuffs.*)

DONNA. Well look what you did now, Jamie.

JAMIE. Look what I did?

DONNA. You got yourself arrested. Who's acting crazy now?

JAMIE. Crazy? You want to see crazy? Officer, I'll help you find 'the zombie.'

OFFICER PERKINS. And why should I let you?

JAMIE. Because I know something you don't know.

OFFICER PERKINS. I failed third grade. You may know several things.

JAMIE. Oh lord.

OFFICER PERKINS. And fifth.

JAMIE. About the zombie specifically.

OFFICER PERKINS. Alright. I want to know that thing.

ELLIE. Yay! The search is on.

OFFICER PERKINS. Wait. First things first. Say you're on the team.

JAMIE. Fine. I'm on the team.

DONNA. You should check the streets. The other apartments. He's definitely not here anymore.

JAMIE. I'm on the team and you're missing something big. Theo wasn't just a man.

OFFICER PERKINS. He was a woman?

JAMIE. He was a leprechaun! He's not just dead. He's un-dead. And a leprechaun.

ELLIE. OH! OH! YES! He's magical. He appears and disappears and it's very shocking but it's very magical.

OFFICER PERKINS. I should call for back up.

JAMIE. NO! Leprechauns can hear all radio transmissions. He'll be one step ahead of us.

OFFICER PERKINS. Can they text?

JAMIE. They invented texting.

OFFICER PERKINS. Oh god. We're in way over our heads. I should call Bart for help –

ELLIE. We can handle this. This is what we know. He is very magical, he has a way of seeing into one's soul that is just impossible to describe, and he is devastatingly attractive.

JAMIE. I wouldn't say devastating.

OFFICER PERKINS. OH NO.

DONNA. What? What happened?

OFFICER PERKINS. Is it possible that he is here right now? In this room?

ELLIE. Is he? Oh my. Theo? Theo? Can you hear me?

JAMIE. He does disappear and reappear without warning.

DONNA. It's always just when you least expect it. He'll just surprise you with a casual compliment and a twinkle of his piercing eyes, then make disturbingly accurate assessment of the way you live your life and work towards your goals.

(There is a knock on the front door. No one moves.)

OFFICER PERKINS. It's Bart. Everyone hide.

*(*JAMIE *opens the door.* **THEO** *has changed into a woman's pant-suit and combed over his hair.)*

THEO. Hello, boy.

OFFICER PERKINS. Who is that?

ELLIE. Who is that?

JAMIE. It's Theo!

DONNA. It's not Theo

THEO. Then who is Theo?

ELLIE. That's not Theo.

DONNA. It's not Theo.

JAMIE. It is.

DONNA. No.

OFFICER PERKINS. Who is it then?

DONNA. This – this is Chaz!

ELLIE. Chaz!

THEO. Yes. I am Chaz. Chaz Bono –

DONNA. Chaz Bonaparte from London. He is staying in Jamie's room for a few months while Jamie is in Chicago.

OFFICER PERKINS. I hate Chicago.

THEO. I've just arrived here in America.

ELLIE. Hi Chaz, I'm Ellie. So excited to have you as our roomie for awhile.

THEO. The pleasure is all mine, beautiful.

ELLIE. Oh hush. You're the beauty.

THEO. Oh stop.

ELLIE. You stop.

THEO. You stop.

DONNA. Both of you stop it right now.

ELLIE. We've heard so much about you. 'Great' things. One story in particular.

THEO. What story is that, deary?

ELLIE. The story of when you and Jamie hooked up.

THEO. When young James and I hooked up. Yes. Our jaunty little experience together on the continent.

JAMIE. We did not. No. Officer, I did not hookup with that.

OFFICER PERKINS. No judgment. I've played on both sides of the street myself, kiddo.

JAMIE. What?

OFFICER PERKINS. People are sexual. Don't over think it.

ELLIE. Chaz, will you say what you said to him that night?

THEO. What I said to him that night?

DONNA. You said –

THEO. OH. Yes. I said "I love you, James."

ELLIE. Shut the front door! Jamie, is this true?

JAMIE. No! No he did not say that.

DONNA. No, Chaz. You didn't say you love Jamie.

THEO. I did. That's why I've come back. To be with James.

OFFICER PERKINS. That is very romantic.

JAMIE. Not romantic. Ew. No. That's not Chaz!

OFFICER PERKINS. Not Chaz?

JAMIE. That's Theo.

OFFICER PERKINS. I thought it was Chaz.

DONNA. It is Chaz.

THEO. I'm Chaz.

OFFICER PERKINS. Are Chaz and Theo similar looking?

ELLIE. Not at all.

DONNA. This is Chaz.

JAMIE. That is Theo.

DONNA. He looks nothing like Theo.

OFFICER PERKINS. I thought Theo was a dead leprechaun.

THEO. Dead?

ELLIE. Theo wore all green. Remember? Theo is Irish. We're both Irish.

DONNA. Theo is from Michigan.

THEO. Chaz is from Brighton.

DONNA. Ellie is from Jacksonville.

OFFICER PERKINS. I'm from Bradenton.

ELLIE. I thought Chaz was from London.

DONNA. No one here is Irish.

ELLIE. Which do you like better, Brighton or London?

THEO. I fancy both.

ELLIE. I'm sure they're both terribly fancy.

JAMIE. You really think that's Chaz?

ELLIE. Look at his suit, Jamie.

JAMIE. I see it. Looks pretty familiar. Cough, Cough Donna.

ELLIE. No American man wears such fine garb. That is an Englishman if I've ever seen one.

THEO. The fashions back West really are years ahead of those in the states.

JAMIE. East.

THEO. Sorry, lover?

JAMIE. Back East. England is east, nitwit.

THEO. Yes, my mistake. I'm Irish originally so I get a bit turned around sometimes.

OFFICER PERKINS. *(motioning in the four cardinal directions)* It's easy to remember if you say Never, Eat, Soggy, Waffles. North, East, South, West.

JAMIE. Ireland is also east.

DONNA. Chaz you're not Irish. You came from England.

THEO. Oh, but I have a castle in Ireland so –

ELLIE. Shut up –

OFFICER PERKINS. – A real castle?

THEO. It's called Blarney Castle. In the middle of nowhere, really. Very hard to find. A family spot.

ELLIE. I wonder if my family has a castle.

JAMIE. Blarney. Castle.

ELLIE. You know it, Jamie?

JAMIE. Everyone knows it, Ellie. It's world famous.

OFFICER PERKINS. You're famous?

JAMIE. He is not famous. He is Theo.

OFFICER PERKINS. That is Chaz. Theo is still deadly and at large.

DONNA. Chaz. This is Chaz. Chaz is here. Theo is not here right now.

ELLIE. Chaz, I'm so sorry, but he is right. It's been a frightful night here. We're actually amidst a crisis.

THEO. A crisis? What terror.

ELLIE. There was a leprechaun here, terribly charming and wonderfully magical, but I am sad to say that he has left this life and moved on to the next.

JAMIE. He has apparently come back as an Englishman in women's clothing.

DONNA. Theo is gone. Gone for good and we should allow this fine police officer to stop searching for him.

ELLIE. We fear Theo may be the first victim of a terrifying plague that allows the dead to walk again.

JAMIE. No one actually fears that, Ellie.

OFFICER PERKINS. I do. I'm sweating. I'm moist.

DONNA. Gross.

ELLIE. Ew.

JAMIE. Gag me.

THEO. You say there is a member the living dead at large and we aren't to be afeard?

ELLIE. Unfortunately we art'uh be afeard.

OFFICER PERKINS. We need to secure the apartment. Split up and search.

DONNA. What will you do when you find Theo, Officer?

OFFICER PERKINS. I will be forced to take him down.

DONNA. Take him down? You can't 'take him down.'

JAMIE. He is standing right there.

DONNA. That is Chaz, Jamie!

THEO. No I'm not.

JAMIE. See!

THEO. Yes I am.

ELLIE. Keep Chaz and Jamie away from each other. The sexual tension in this scenario is pretty extreme.

THEO. Don't deny it, James.

ELLIE. I'll stick with Officer Melvin.

OFFICER PERKINS. That's not my name. It's. Perkins. Verne Perkins.

DONNA. Verne? What kind of a name is Verne?

ELLIE. Verne, we'll check my room and Jamie's room. Donna and Chaz you get the bathroom and Donna's room. Jamie, you check every nook and cranny in here. Okay. Hands in.

I want everyone to stay focused. ZLH on three. One, two, three – Zombie-Lepresaurus Hunters!

> (**ELLIE** and **OFFICER PERKINS** exit through door #2. **DONNA** and **JAMIE** remain in the living room.)

JAMIE. Donna, I swear if this doesn't end soon I'm going to lose my mind.

DONNA. I know. I know. I have no idea what's even going on anymore.

THEO. I'm Chaz, Theo is dead and came back to life after being hit by a zombie, Verne –

JAMIE. Shut up!

DONNA. Don't make a scene.

JAMIE. Me make a scene?

DONNA. I want it to stop too!

THEO. I'm thirsty.

DONNA. There is beer in the fridge.

THEO. Yummo.

JAMIE. No. No more beer. No more coffee. Stop.

DONNA. Let him have the beer. Maybe he'll pass out again and sleep til morning when we can figure out how he got in here.

JAMIE. I don't care how he got in.

THEO. I forgot my keys.

JAMIE. You've got to help me stop this. You're losing it.

DONNA. I don't want Theo getting arrested. It's making me do crazy things.

JAMIE. He deserves to be arrested.

DONNA. Look at him with that beer. He looks like a baby with his bottle.

JAMIE. Awww, so cute.

THEO. I'm cute.

JAMIE. No. You're a creepy breaking-in drug addict.

DONNA. It's not his fault.

THEO. I was standing in line for the bathroom and –

JAMIE. That's not real.

DONNA. He's in fashion. He's a good guy. Haven't you ever done coke while you were drunk?

JAMIE. I have never done coke period. Have you?

DONNA. No. He must be so scared.

JAMIE. He is fine. He is acting British now for god's sake.

THEO. Fancy a snog?

DONNA. Brilliant right?

JAMIE. Not brilliant. This is a mess.

DONNA. It's up to us to clean it up.

JAMIE. I hate you.

DONNA. We just need to get Chaz out of here –

JAMIE. It's Theo.

DONNA. Theo out of here so you and I can figure out how to get Verne out of here.

JAMIE. Even if we can get Theo to leave how are we going to get Verne to let all of this zombie drama go?

DONNA. Verne really thinks there is a zombie running around.

JAMIE. Stupid idiot rookie cop.

DONNA. A a terrified rookie mess and I don't want someone getting shot.

JAMIE. Amen. You get rid of Theo, I'll distract those dingbats.

(JAMIE *goes into door #2.*)

DONNA. Theo, I need to get you out of the apartment.

THEO. I drank my beer is all gone. It's always the nightcap that does ya in for bad. Will you help me stand up, beauty?

DONNA. Come here.

> (**DONNA** *helps* **THEO** *stand up. He hugs her and she embraces him. They kiss.*)

You really are magical.

THEO. You give me too much credit.

DONNA. Oh stop.

THEO. I don't even know how this happened.

DONNA. How what happened?

THEO. Us. There are so many factors working against us but somehow we found each other. You're here and I'm here and we're together. I feel happy. You're very beautiful.

DONNA. Theo. You're unreal. Like. What? Ugh. Kiss me.

THEO. Okay.

> (*They kiss.*)

DONNA. Thank you.

THEO. My little model.

DONNA. I told you I don't model. Listen, before you leave I need to tell you something.

THEO. I'm not good at keeping secrets.

DONNA. I took your advice. I quit my job. I took your advice. You told me to leap and the net would appear. It was poetic and I heard it. I've basically been saying it to myself this whole time. It was scary but I leapt.

THEO. Wow. You did that because of me?

DONNA. I did it because of me – but you helped me trust myself. I was an assistant but I'm going to be an actual lawyer. It's amazing.

THEO. You're so pretty. I could love you.

DONNA. That would be nice.

OFFICER PERKINS. *(offstage)* I AM A STRONG CONFIDENT officer AND I AM IN CONTROL OF THIS SITUATION AND MY FEELINGS.

DONNA. Okay. We have to get you home, Theo. Verne is a little – in the head. I don't want anyone figuring out that you –

THEO. I've got an idea!

(*THEO runs into door #1 and slams it.*)

DONNA. Crap! JAMIE! Oh poopy.

(*JAMIE comes out of door #2.*)

JAMIE. What? Is he gone? Oh good. Thank god. Verne is really losing it. They are having a talk about his feelings.

DONNA. He locked himself in my room again.

JAMIE. I hate him. Let's take this opportunity to get off the Zombie thing and get Verne out of here. It's freaking me out. Such a spazz.

DONNA. Fine.

JAMIE & DONNA. Ellie!

DONNA. What's the plan?

JAMIE. Uh — We'll tell them we saw on the news that they caught the zombie and tell Verne to leave. Done and done.

DONNA. BoopBoop here we go!

(*ELLIE and OFFICER PERKINS come out of door #2.*)

ELLIE. Sorry for the delay. Verne and I were having a discussion. Verne, is there anything you would like to share with the group?

(*ELLIE hands OFFICER PERKINS the talking stick.*)

OFFICER PERKINS. I'm – I would – I had a rough childhood. Three older brothers and my mother died when I was nine –

JAMIE. I don't have time for all that. Verne, we just saw the news. They caught the Zombie and they are asking all police to report back to headquarters. Thank you for your help. KThanksBye. Goodnight.

(**THEO** *comes out of door #1 and is once again dressed as a leprechaun. No one sees him.*)

ELLIE. Was Theo really arrested? That's terrible.

OFFICER PERKINS. That's victory. Justice in the name of the law.

THEO. I'm not arrested.

ELLIE. BAH! HAHA!

OFFICER PERKINS. Le-Le-Le-Leprechaun!

JAMIE. BAH! Oh Oh Oh –

DONNA. AH!

OFFICER PERKINS. Get him!

THEO. You'll never get me gold!

(**THEO** *runs through the living room. After a brief chase, he uses* **DONNA** *as a shield.* **ELLIE** *and* **OFFICER PERKINS** *are trying to trap him.*)

ELLIE. Theo! Stop. We're not going to hurt you.

DONNA. Theo. You're back. What happened to Chaz?

OFFICER PERKINS. I am an officer of the law and I need you to put your face over your head and keep your back behind your arms.

THEO. Chaz split his pants and got the train back to England for a new one.

OFFICER PERKINS. Hands in the air.

JAMIE. Can everyone calm down for a second.

THEO. I'm really dizzy.

ELLIE. If there is any part of you still alive in there we need you to listen. It's Dr. Ellie Vandam and we have to quarantine you as soon as possible before the virus infects the entire eastern seaboard.

DONNA. Where do you live? Let me take you home.

OFFICER PERKINS. Don't you dare. I am the police.

(**OFFICER PERKINS** *pulls out a gun.*)

DONNA. Don't you point that thing at me!

OFFICER PERKINS. I'm pointing at the monster.

JAMIE. You're going to hurt someone.

OFFICER PERKINS. Things here are completely out of control. Completely out of control.

ELLIE. Verne. Put down the gun. Let me handle this.

OFFICER PERKINS. I won't be eaten by a zombie! No one leaves this room.

JAMIE. This has gone too far.

ELLIE. It has. We can stop now. Verne, –

OFFICER PERKINS. I really think the best thing to do here is to –

ELLIE. Do not shoot!

OFFICER PERKINS. I think I'm going to shoot.

JAMIE. Do not shoot!

DONNA. Don't shoot!

OFFICER PERKINS. I have to.

THEO. No please.

OFFICER PERKINS. Yes. I've got to.

ELLIE. Wait, Verne, he's not –

OFFICER PERKINS. I'm shooting –

ELLIE. It's all a joke –

DONNA. Please don't –

JAMIE. Verne!

> (**THEO** *screams and he runs around* **DONNA** *towards* **OFFICER PERKINS**.)

THEO. AHHH!

ELLIE. AHHH!

OFFICER PERKINS. AHHH!

> (As **THEO** *runs at* **OFFICER PERKINS**, *the gun fires and everyone falls to the floor. For a brief moment there is absolutely no movement. Suddenly,* **THEO** *springs up and runs out the front door.*)

> (**DONNA, JAMIE, OFFICER PERKINS**, *and* **ELLIE** *begin to move.*)

ELLIE. Are we dead?

DONNA. I'm not dead.

OFFICER PERKINS. Did I get him? The Zombrechaun?

DONNA. Oh my friggin' god. Theo?

OFFICER PERKINS. Did we win?

DONNA. No. Where is Theo?

JAMIE. This is hell.

ELLIE. This was fun and fantastical but now –

DONNA. Theo left again.

ELLIE. I'm not having fun anymore.

OFFICER PERKINS. This was never about fun.

ELLIE. Verne, I'm not normally one to get angry but – Are you out of your mind?! Of course it was fun! Do you really think that, if there was a member of the undead in my apartment, I would be here searching for him? I'd hightail my butt to Roosevelt Island with a shotgun and a carton of Parliaments. That leprechaun is just a ridiculous drunk dude that doesn't really know where he is.

DONNA. And we don't know where he came from.

JAMIE. Or how he got into the apartment.

DONNA. How he keeps getting into the apartment.

ELLIE. How does he keep doing that? We don't know. That's the whole point of the story!

OFFICER PERKINS. What story? Why did you let me believe – this is all some game to you?

ELLIE. I do it all the time.

DONNA. She really does.

JAMIE. You get used to it eventually.

OFFICER PERKINS. Officers of the law are not pawns to played with.

ELLIE. You made it pretty easy.

JAMIE. "Officer of the law" is being generous I think.

ELLIE. It's your first day.

DONNA. How did you end up here by yourself on your first day?

OFFICER PERKINS. My partner is downstairs in the car and said I could handle it.

JAMIE. You handled it.

DONNA. Our system is so screwed up.

OFFICER PERKINS. You abused the system.

JAMIE. You have no idea what you're doing.

OFFICER PERKINS. I'm trying.

ELLIE. Verne, it's time for you to go.

OFFICER PERKINS. But – The leprechaun –

ELLIE. He's a man, Verne. A man. A man of fiction and whimsy.

OFFICER PERKINS. A man.

DONNA. I think we can handle things from here.

OFFICER PERKINS. There wasn't ever an intruder at all? No possible death, assault, drug use, infidelity?

JAMIE. Verne, just go.

*(**OFFICER PERKINS** takes a walk of shame towards the front door.)*

OFFICER PERKINS. Dialing 911 without actual need for police or medical assistance is against the law in all fifty states –

ELLIE. Verne, –

OFFICER PERKINS. I wouldn't have come if I –

ELLIE. Verne, –

OFFICER PERKINS. Please don't tell anyone about the gun.

ELLIE. Goodnight, Verne.

OFFICER PERKINS. Good morning.

*(**OFFICER PERKINS** exits.)*

JAMIE. Is it over yet?

DONNA. Do you think he'll come back again?

ELLIE. Verne?

DONNA. Theo.

ELLIE. Right. Sorry. Wow, I just felt my hangover start. What happened to Chaz?

DONNA. We're not doing this again.

JAMIE. I'm just happy he's gone.

DONNA. I'm not.

JAMIE. That's right. You're in love.

DONNA. Shut up, Jamie.

> (*There is a knock at the front door.*)

THEO. (*offstage*) Help.

> (**DONNA** *opens the door.*)

DONNA. Theo!

THEO. Ouchies.

  I got shot.

> (**THEO** *faints.*)

ELLIE. He might actually be dead this time. He's bleeding a lot. His arm is shot.

DONNA. Theo, wake up –

ELLIE. Jamie, get me a pillow and a tie.

> (**JAMIE** *goes.*)

  Donna, get my suture kit from the top drawer of my desk.

DONNA. Why do you have a –

ELLIE. Do you want him to die?

> (**DONNA** *goes.* **ELLIE** *kneels over* **THEO** *and checks his pulse. She tears the sleeve off his costume.* **JAMIE** *re-enters.*)

JAMIE. Here.

ELLIE. Give me the Tie. Put the pillow under his head.

JAMIE. What are you doing?

ELLIE. Making a tourniquet.

JAMIE. Is he okay?

ELLIE. I don't know. He's bleeding a lot and I can't really see the wound. Jamie, call 911.

JAMIE. Oh crap.

> (**DONNA** *re-enters with kit and gives it to* **ELLIE.** **THEO** *starts waking up.* **JAMIE** *calls 911.*)

DONNA. Kit! Here.

THEO. Ouchies.

ELLIE. Theo. We're going to take good care of you, okay?

THEO. Get off!

ELLIE. Donna, hold him down.

JAMIE. Hi. I need an ambulance.

ELLIE. Hold him still!

DONNA. Theo, stay calm. We're going to help you. We have to stop the bleeding.

THEO. I want to go to bed.

ELLIE. Oh. This isn't that bad.

DONNA. Where is home?

THEO. Here.

ELLIE. Bloody but not that bad.

DONNA. This isn't your home, Theo.

THEO.	**JAMIE.**
30 –17 23rd ave.	30 –17 23rd ave.
Apartment 6	Apartment 4

ELLIE. I've never been so scared in my life. Except when Verne shot Theo.

JAMIE. Yes, Ma'am. That's the right address.

DONNA. Not the right apartment.

ELLIE. Jamie, remember when Verne shot Theo? Oh. You can hang up. It's not that bad.

JAMIE. Yes, ma'am it's us again.

ELLIE. Just hang up he's fine.

THEO. I have the big room.

DONNA. Do you live in this building?

JAMIE. Never mind. He's fine. Don't send an ambulance.

THEO. I forgot my keys.

JAMIE. He's still wasted but whatever. Goodnight. Bye.

(JAMIE *hangs up.*)

DONNA. Do you live in this friggin' building?

THEO. Ouch!

ELLIE. A running whipstitch to save. your. life!

DONNA. You were trying to get into your apartment. You crawled in through the window.

THEO. I forgot my keys.

DONNA. Yes!

JAMIE. I don't get it.

DONNA. We figured out the Theo mystery! He came in through my window. Climbed up the fire escape and then he came in through my window because he thought he was crawling in his window. He came from behind me and I thought it was her and when I put him in your room my door was open. I always shut my door. He came in my window.

ELLIE. Did you come in the window?

THEO. Do it all the time when I'm locked out.

JAMIE. You don't live here!

THEO. Stop yelling at me.

JAMIE. I'm taking you upstairs.

ELLIE. Wait! I'm almost done.

DONNA. Jamie, back off. Come on, Theo. Stand up for me and we'll get you home.

THEO. You're the prettiest.

ELLIE. Keep pressure on the wound until the bleeding stops. You're going to make it.

THEO. My head hurts.

ELLIE. You should keep him awake in case he has a concussion or a hematoma.

THEO. Goodnight, girl.

ELLIE. Goodnight, Theo.

THEO. Hate you, boy.

JAMIE. Go kill yourself, addict.

THEO. It was cokerape!

JAMIE. That's not a real thing.

(*DONNA and* **THEO** *exit.*)

ELLIE. Totally using it in the book.

JAMIE. Can you die of sleep deprivation?

ELLIE. You're not going to die.

JAMIE. Promise?

ELLIE. Sure. Promise. How's your hand?

JAMIE. I don't recommend punching people.

ELLIE. You shouldn't have done that.

JAMIE. There are a lot things we shouldn't have done tonight. Donna is going to wake up tomorrow with some serious regrets.

ELLIE. She's having a weird night.

JAMIE. She's always having a weird night or a rough day or a hard week at work. She's irrationally discontent and it's making her act like an idiot.

ELLIE. She didn't let Theo in and don't call her an idiot.

JAMIE. I'm putting my foot down before she starts inviting the heroin addicts from St. Marks over for a mixer.

(*DONNA comes back in the apartment and slams the door. She grabs herself a beer and sits down with* **ELLIE** *and* **JAMIE**.)

Find his apartment?

DONNA. Yep.

JAMIE. He went inside?

DONNA. Roommate let him in.

ELLIE. Poor guy.

JAMIE. He probably won't remember any of this.

DONNA. He doesn't.

ELLIE. Doesn't?

DONNA. Remember me.

JAMIE. He just left.

DONNA. He already forgot.

ELLIE. He couldn't have –

DONNA. He did. Roomie opened the door and he was like "whaaaaat?"

JAMIE. I told you.

(One last time, **THEO** enters through door #1.)

DONNA. I feel so weird all over my body.

ELLIE. You're in shock. It was a crazy night.

JAMIE. She quit her job. That's a big change.

DONNA. I'm proud of that. Theo was right.

THEO. I'm always right.

JAMIE. AHH!

ELLIE. WAHHHHAHAHAHA. Oh my god. How do you keep doing that? I can't. I'm terrified but I can't stop laughing.

DONNA. Theo.

THEO. Donnie.

DONNA. You came back. You came back for me?

THEO. Once more down the fire escape. I have something to say.

JAMIE. We're calling Steve and having the locks on those windows changed first thing tomorrow.

DONNA. What is it, Theo?

THEO. I –

DONNA. Yes?

THEO. I –

(A knock at the door.)

OFFICER BART. (offstage) Open up! This is the police. I'm looking for Officer Perkins.

JAMIE. This can't be happening again.

ELLIE. Verne?

THEO. I can't get shot again.

DONNA. No one is getting shot. Stay.

OFFICER BART. *(offstage)* Yes. Verne. Rookie Cop. Sweats a lot.

THEO. My wife said I should come down and say sorry and come right home.

DONNA. I understand.

THEO. I'm really sorry.

DONNA. Wait, what? Wife? What?

THEO. I'm sorry.

DONNA. You have a wife?

OFFICER BART. *(offstage)* Hello? I don't have time for dramatic revelations.

DONNA. You got smoochy smoochy with me.

THEO. Sorry!

DONNA. You gave me advice and said that you loved me.

THEO. Sorry!

JAMIE. I'll knock him out again.

DONNA. Jamie, I've got this.

THEO. Little Twerp.

DONNA. Don't call him a twerp, you skeeze!

THEO. Sorry, Donnie.

OFFICER BART. *(offstage)* Open up!

DONNA. Be right there, officer. We've got the guy right here. Theodore Forbes McGuintilly. Broke into my house.

THEO. Donnie! You're going to get me in trouble.

DONNA. Donna. My name is Donna!

JAMIE. Theo, you better run because she might actually kill you.

(THEO runs out door #1.)

DONNA, ELLIE, JAMIE. —

DONNA. Can you believe that?

JAMIE. I knew it. I knew he was a sneaky snake.

DONNA. You were right.

ELLIE. What a bummer.

DONNA. —

JAMIE. I think we need to open the door now.

DONNA. Hold on. Let me get my coffee first.

OFFICER BART. *(offstage)* Verne?

DONNA. Coming!

JAMIE. Let's just keep this short.

ELLIE. Another chapter begins. How riveting.

DONNA. Okay. Let's do this. Shit.

      (Lights out.)

End of Play